The Homestead
A to Z

by Katie Hines Porterfield
Art by Courtney Sievers

ACKNOWLEDGMENTS

First and foremost, I'd like to extend a heartfelt
thank you to The Omni Homestead Resort. I am also
extremely grateful for the talented and dedicated
Courtney Sievers, the irreplaceable Circa Design team,
and my patient Mascot Books editor, Kristin Perry.

The Homestead A to Z

Copyright ©2018 Katie Hines Porterfield

Art by Courtney Sievers
Art Direction and Book Design by Circa Design

For more information, please contact:
Mascot Books
620 Herndon Parkway, Suite 320
Herndon, VA 20170
info@mascotbooks.com

Library of Congress Control Number: 2018955545

CPSIA Code: PRT0918A
ISBN-13: 978-1-64307-101-5

Printed in the United States

To my mother-in-law and father-in-law, Charlotte and Bittle Porterfield (a.k.a. Gaga & G-Daddy to their grandsons). Thank you for introducing Forrest, and, in turn, me and, later, our children, to this special place. We cherish our Homestead memories. From our "meet the parents" weekend to our wedding engagement to holidays, hikes, Main Dining Room dinners, your dining room dinners, grill time, father-mother-son golf, cousin-golf, and hours at the pool, Forrest and I wouldn't trade anything for these moments and countless others marked by time spent with family in this spectacular backdrop.

-Katie

Thank you to my son, Witten, for helping me see the world through the eyes of a child again to create these paintings. You inspire me and make me so proud. Always be the best you can be. Also, thank you to my parents and husband for your love and support. It has meant the world. Much love.

-Courtney

Nestled in the Alleghenies in a town called Hot Springs,
this old Virginia resort is truly fit for kings.

Presidents have walked its halls and scenic grounds,
and families like yours have really made the rounds.

Guests come when the lawn is green or even covered with snow.
They know as well as I do there's no bad time to go.

And when their stay is over, I often hear them say,
"There's no place like the Homestead—we'll come again one day."

So, join me and I'll show you all there is to do and see.
We'll reminisce a bit, as we explore from A to Z.

Did you know I'm the official state bird of Virginia?

Look for me on every page!

Shoot an arrow at the **A**rchery range.

Ride a **B**ike on a trail for a change.

Canoe the Jackson at any pace.

Pick which **D**uck will win the race.

Where is your
favorite place to **E**at?

Mastering Falconry is quite the feat.

Play miniature **G**olf or try a real course.

Take a carriage ride or hop on a **H**orse.

Ice skating in the winter is pretty cool.

Soak with your family in the Jefferson Pool.

Croquet or corn hole on the big green Lawn?

Stop by Martha's Market
for a treat or two.

Hiking with the Naturalist is a must-do.

Oh, what fun it is to watch kids splash and play.

Penguin Slides Tubing Park
is for a colder day.

Quiet in the halls,
keep voices low.

The **R**ed tail racer
is ready to go.

Skiing and Snowboarding are fun for all.

A big Christmas Tree lights up the Great Hall.

How many fish do you see Under there?

Downtime for Video games is pretty rare.

The **W**ashington Library has games as well.

X marks the spot of this one-of-a-kind hotel.

Yikes! It's dark in the tube water slide!

Let's catch some
Zzz's
I'm a tired tour guide.

AUTHOR

Katie Hines Porterfield

A writer based in Nashville, Tennessee, Katie Hines Porterfield holds a B.A. in American Studies from the University of the South and an M.A. in Journalism from the University of Alabama. Her first book, *Sewanee A to Z*, which was published in 2014, launched her business, A to Z Children's Books. Today, her growing brand of books includes *Find Your Heart in Lake Martin: An A to Z Book* and *The Sewanee Night Before Christmas*. Keep an eye out for *Smith Lake A to Z*, coming soon! She and her husband, Forrest, are the proud parents of twin boys, Hines and Shep. You can purchase her books and see more of her work at atozchildrensbooks.com.

ARTIST

Courtney Sievers

Courtney Sievers is an expressive artist living in Richmond, Virginia, with her husband and son. She began her painting career at Mary Baldwin College earning a degree in Fine Art and Art Education in 1998. Her style is colorful and expressive, and she loves creating images that evoke a happy mood or memory for somebody.

To Courtney, inspiration is everywhere: clouds in the brilliant blue sky, morning sunlight hitting a tree, all the gorgeous flowers growing around us, the beauty and power of water. The list can go on and on! To her, the abundance of color nature provides is simply amazing. The best part for Courtney is expressing her awe of it on canvas. Movement, texture, and color are so exciting for her to create!

In Richmond, you'll find her in her home studio in the Fan District working on new pieces for galleries and commissions. When she is not painting, she enjoys being with family and friends, decorating her home, gardening, and she especially loves going to the beach! You can view her work at courtneysievers.com.